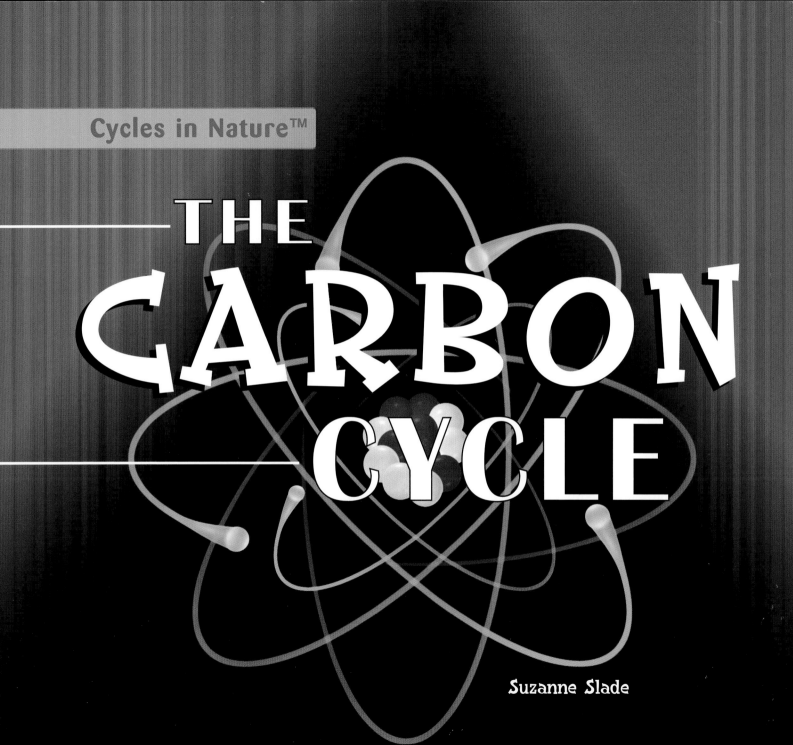

Cycles in Nature™

THE CARBON CYCLE

Suzanne Slade

To the ever-encouraging, super-smiley Mrs. Fiedler and all the other outstanding teachers at Highland Middle School

Published in 2007 by The Rosen Publishing Group, Inc.
29 East 21st Street, New York, NY 10010

First Edition

Editor: Joanne Randolph
Book Design: Greg Tucker
Photo Researcher: Amy Feinberg

Illustrations: p. 13 by Michelle Innes.
Photo Credits: Cover, p. 4 © Don Farrall/Photodisc Green/Getty Images; p. 5 © Kaj R. Svensson/Science Photo Library/Photo Researchers, Inc.; p. 6 © Robert Landau/Corbis; p. 7 www.istockphoto.com/Paul Topp; p. 8 NASA-GSFC; p. 9 © University Corporation for Atmospheric Research; p. 10 © Alfred Pasieka/Science Photo Library/Photo Researchers, Inc.; p. 11 © Edward Hattersley/Alamy; p. 12 © Lucidio Studio, Inc./Corbis; p. 14 © Andre Jenny/The Image Works; p. 15 © Véronique Estiot/Photo Researchers, Inc.; p. 16 © Dr. Tim Evans/Science Photo Library/Photo Researchers, Inc.; p. 17 © JLP/Deimos/zefa/Corbis; p. 18 © George Steinmetz/Corbis; p. 19 © Louie Psihoyos/Corbis; p. 20 © Steve Cole/Photodisc Green/Getty Images; p. 21 © Natalie Fobes/Corbis.

Library of Congress Cataloging-in-Publication Data

Slade, Suzanne.
  The carbon cycle / Suzanne Slade.— 1st ed.
    p. cm. — (Cycles in nature)
  Includes index.
  ISBN 1-4042-3490-X (library binding) — ISBN 1-4042-2199-9 (pbk.) — ISBN 1-4042-2389-4 (six pack)
  1. Carbon—Juvenile literature. 2. Cycles—Juvenile literature. I. Title. II. Series: Cycles in nature (Rosen Pub. Group's PowerKids Press)

QD181.C1S58 2007
546'.681—dc22

                                            2005035819

Manufactured in the United States of America

Contents

What Is Carbon?   4

Carbon Compounds   6

Carbon Moves in a Cycle   8

Carbon in the Air   10

Carbon in Plants   12

Carbon in Animals   14

Two Paths   16

Fossil Fuels   18

Upsetting the Cycle   20

The Carbon Cycle in Our World   22

Glossary   23

Index   24

Web Sites   24

What Is Carbon?

Carbon is one of about 90 natural **elements** in the world. Elements are the basic building blocks that make everything. The stars, Earth, air, and even your body are made of carbon and other elements.

Every element is made of tiny **particles** called **atoms**. Atoms are so small you cannot see them. Atoms are made of three smaller particles called **protons**, **neutrons**, and **electrons**. Often atoms of different elements bond together to create new things. A bond is

This is a carbon atom. Carbon has six electrons that spin around its nucleus, or center. The nucleus is made of protons and neutrons. Carbon is the sixth-most-common element in the world.

formed between atoms when they share or give electrons to each other.

Every element has its own **symbol** of one, two, or three letters. The symbol for carbon is the letter *C*. All the elements and their symbols are listed on a chart called the periodic table.

Cycle Facts

Carbon has many different appearances. For example, a beautiful shiny rock called a diamond and a black piece of coal are both made of carbon. Your pencil lead also has a soft and slippery form of carbon called graphite in it.

Carbon Compounds

What do you have in common with a tree, your pet hamster, and a butterfly? Carbon is found in your body and in every other living thing, including trees, hamsters, and butterflies. Carbon makes up almost 20 **percent** of your body. So if you weigh 80 pounds (36 kg), your body would have about 16 pounds (7 kg) of carbon.

All living things are made with carbon. Living things also need carbon compounds to stay

One carbon compound is carbon monoxide. This is a harmful gas for people and animals to breathe. Shown here is a city with polluted air, called smog. Smog has a lot of carbon monoxide. Smog is created by the burning of fuels that have carbon or by gases given off by cars and trucks.

alive. A carbon compound is formed when carbon atoms join with atoms of other elements. Carbon compounds can be in the form of a solid, liquid, or gas. Carbon atoms join with other elements easily. In fact scientists have discovered more than eight million carbon compounds. Carbon is found in more compounds than any other element.

This butterfly has carbon in its body. It takes in carbon compounds when it gets its food from plants, too.

Cycle Facts

Places where carbon is stored for a long time are called sinks. Carbon sinks include trees, a rock called limestone, and places where dead plants or animals are buried.

Carbon Moves in a Cycle

Earth and the air have only a certain amount of carbon. This carbon moves through nature in a cycle. A cycle is a pattern that happens again and again. In the carbon cycle, the limited amount of carbon on Earth is reused in many forms by all living things.

The carbon cycle begins when plants take in carbon compounds from the air. When animals eat plants, they take in carbon from the plants. The cycle is complete when animals put carbon back into the air by breathing out carbon

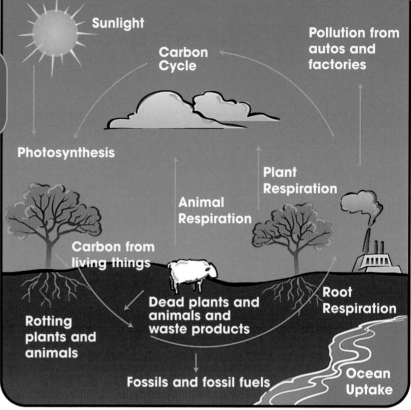

This picture shows the carbon cycle in action. Every time a plant dies or a person breathes, the carbon cycle continues.

compounds. Some carbon stored in plants and animals also goes into the earth when they die. Every living thing uses and creates carbon compounds in the carbon cycle. For millions of years, carbon has moved through this endless cycle.

Cycle Facts

There are about 750 billion tons (680 billion t) of carbon in the air surrounding Earth. One billion is a very large number.

Carbon in the Air

Carbon moves through the air in the form of gases. The most common carbon compound gas is called carbon dioxide. People and animals make carbon dioxide gas when they breathe.

Carbon dioxide is made of two elements, carbon and **oxygen**. Scientists use a formula to show which elements join together to make up a compound. The formula for carbon dioxide is CO_2. A formula also shows how many atoms of each element are in one

Oxygen

Carbon

This is a carbon dioxide molecule. The carbon atom is in the center. The two oxygen atoms have bonded with the carbon to form CO_2.

molecule. A molecule is the smallest part of a compound. The *C* in carbon dioxide's formula means there is one carbon atom in a molecule of carbon dioxide. The small two beside the *O* means there are two oxygen atoms in the molecule.

Cycle Facts

Carbon dioxide is found in soft drinks. The bubbles in your soda are tiny pockets of carbon dioxide gas.

Carbon + Oxygen $\longrightarrow$ Carbon Dioxide

$$C + O_2 \longrightarrow CO_2$$

This scientific equation shows how a molecule of carbon dioxide is formed.

Carbon in Plants

In the carbon cycle, plants take carbon from the air and use it to grow. Many plants get carbon from the carbon dioxide gas they take in through tiny holes in their leaves called stomata. Using a **process** called **photosynthesis**, plants use carbon dioxide, sunlight, and water to make food. Plants make a food called **glucose** during photosynthesis. It takes six atoms of carbon to make one molecule of the carbon compound called glucose. Plants use glucose for **energy** to

This plant has just begun to grow. Plants need the right amount of light, water, soil, and carbon dioxide in order to live and grow.

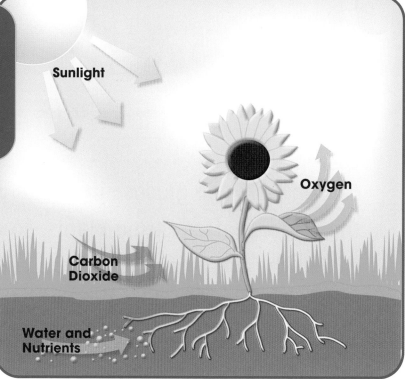

This picture shows how photosynthesis works. The plant takes in sunlight and carbon dioxide through its leaves. It takes in water through its roots. A change takes place in the leaves when the sunlight, carbon dioxide, water, and matter called chlorophyll mix. This creates glucose and oxygen. The plant uses the glucose for food and puts the oxygen back into the air.

Sunlight

Oxygen

Carbon Dioxide

Water and Nutrients

grow. Without glucose, plants could not make stems, leaves, needles, flowers, fruits, vegetables, or other parts.

During photosynthesis plants also give off oxygen gas. People and animals need to breathe oxygen gas to stay alive. In turn people and animals use oxygen to create the carbon dioxide plants need.

Cycle Facts

During winter some parts of the world get less sunlight and become very cold. Some plants stop photosynthesis for a few months due to these changes in the weather.

Carbon in Animals

The carbon cycle continues as animals eat plants and take in carbon from the glucose in plants. Animals store some carbon in their bodies after eating plants, so animals also get carbon from eating the meat of other animals. The hamburger you ate for lunch, for example, gives your body carbon.

Animals use a process called respiration to move the carbon in their bodies back into the air. During respiration animals breathe in oxygen. This oxygen is used to oxidize, or burn, glucose. When

These cattle are taking in carbon compounds as they graze, or eat grass.

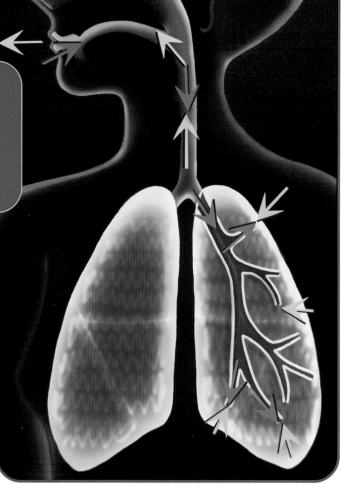

This picture shows how respiration works. As a person breathes in, he or she brings oxygen into the lungs. The lungs share the oxygen with a person's blood, which carries the oxygen to parts of the body that need it. As the body uses the oxygen up, carbon dioxide is created. This is carried back to the lungs by the blood and then breathed back out of the body.

glucose burns, it turns into carbon dioxide and energy. Your body needs energy to move, grow, keep your heart beating, and do many other things. After animals breathe carbon dioxide into the air, plants use the carbon dioxide for photosynthesis.

Cycle Facts

People breathe out about 8 billion tons (7 billion t) of carbon dioxide each year.

Two Paths

Carbon moves through two paths in the carbon cycle. In both paths carbon begins as carbon dioxide and enters plants through photosynthesis. In the **carbohydrate** path, carbon moves between plants and animals in compounds called carbohydrates. Carbohydrates are foods, such as glucose, that give plants and animals energy.

In the **protein** path of the carbon cycle, animals take carbon from the plants and animals they eat in compounds called proteins. Your

This is a model of glucose. Glucose is a carbon compound created by plants during photosynthesis. People also use glucose for energy.

body uses proteins to grow and fix itself and for energy. In the final part of the protein path, carbon goes into the earth when an animal dies and its body decays, or rots. During this process a body slowly breaks down into its basic elements and carbon is put into the earth. Carbon dioxide also goes into the air during decay.

When you eat meat, such as a hamburger, you are taking in proteins. Proteins help your body grow and stay healthy and strong. When you eat carbohydrates, such as the bun on this sandwich, you are giving your body energy. Imagine how you would feel without these important carbon compounds!

Cycle Facts

Protein molecules are different from carbohydrates because they also have atoms of an element called nitrogen. There are a huge number of different kinds of proteins. Meat has many different kinds of proteins your body needs. Your hair and blood are made of different proteins.

Fossil Fuels

The world gets most of its energy from **fossil fuels**. Fossil fuels form deep inside the earth. Over time the bodies of plants and animals that have died break down and sink down into the earth. After millions of years, these bodies, including those of dinosaurs, become fossil fuels. Fossil fuels are rich in carbon from decayed plants and animals.

The three basic fossil fuels are oil, coal, and natural gas. Oil is used to make the liquid gas we put in our cars.

Here oil is being taken from where it is stored beneath Earth's surface. It will be used as fuel for heat and electricity for our homes and gas for our cars.

This is a fossil of Coelophysis, which is a dinosaur that lived 215 to 222 million years ago. Fossils are the remains or imprints of plants or animals that died long ago. Fossil fuels are created when plants and animals break down into their basic compounds over a very long time. We are then able to use the carbon that is left behind.

Electricity for our homes is made in power plants from oil and coal. Some people use natural gas to heat their homes and cook food. When a fossil fuel burns, the carbon in the fuel joins with oxygen atoms in the air to create carbon dioxide gas.

Cycle Facts

Scientists believe that most of the oil and coal stored in the ground was formed about 280 to 345 million years ago. They call that time in Earth's history the Carboniferous period.

Upsetting the Cycle

The carbon cycle has been in balance for millions of years. Today scientists are concerned that people are upsetting that cycle. The world uses fossil fuels for heat, electricity, and running cars. Burning fossil fuels creates a large amount of carbon dioxide. People are also cutting down forests to make room for towns and farms. During photosynthesis trees use carbon dioxide to make oxygen, providing balance in the carbon cycle.

Many scientists believe too much carbon dioxide is harming

The waste from cars and trucks creates harmful carbon compounds, such as carbon monoxide. These carbon compounds pollute the air and make it unsafe to breathe.

our atmosphere. The atmosphere is a mixture of gases that surrounds Earth. Earth's atmosphere acts like a blanket. It keeps some of Earth's heat from escaping into space. As the atmosphere collects more carbon dioxide, it holds in more of Earth's heat. Some scientists believe Earth is slowly getting warmer. This is called global warming.

Cutting down forests is one way people are upsetting the carbon cycle. Trees store carbon as they take in carbon dioxide to make food. They also are an important way that people get oxygen. When large numbers of trees are cut down, there is more carbon dioxide in the air and less oxygen created.

Cycle Facts

Every year people put 6 billion tons (5 billion t) of carbon in the air by burning fossil fuels.

The Carbon Cycle in Our World

Carbon has been cycling through our world since the beginning of time. In nature carbon combines with other elements to create many compounds. These carbon compounds help carbon move through the carbon cycle.

Scientists have also created compounds in labs, called **synthetic** compounds. Many synthetic compounds made with carbon have become an important part of our lives. We use the synthetic carbon compound called plastic every day. Plastic bottles hold foods, such as milk, peanut butter, and ketchup. Video games are played with plastic controls. We even wear clothes made of plastic cloth called polyester.

Carbon is an important element in our world. All living things have carbon. Living things also depend on carbon as it cycles through the air, plants, animals, and the earth to stay alive.

Cycle Facts

One plastic made with carbon, called kevlar, is stronger than steel. Kevlar is also lighter than steel and is used to make parts for airplanes.

Glossary

atoms (A-temz) The smallest parts of elements that can exist either alone or with other elements.

carbohydrate (kar-boh-HY-drayt) The main element in foods, such as bread, made mostly from plants.

electrons (ih-LEK-tronz) Particles inside atoms that spin around the center of an atom.

elements (EH-luh-ments) The basic matter of which all things are made.

energy (EH-nur-jee) The power to work or to act.

fossil (FAH-sul) The hardened remains of a dead animal or plant.

fuels (FYOOLZ) Things used to make energy, warmth, or power.

glucose (GLOO-kohs) The sugar that plants and animals make and use for energy.

molecule (MAH-lih-kyool) Two or more atoms joined together.

neutrons (NOO-tronz) Particles with no electric charge found in the center of an atom.

oxygen (OK-sih-jen) A gas that has no color, taste, or odor and is necessary for people and animals to breathe.

particles (PAR-tih-kulz) Small pieces of matter.

percent (pur-SENT) One part of 100.

photosynthesis (foh-toh-SIN-thuh-sus) The process in which green plants make their own food from sunlight, water, and a gas called carbon dioxide.

process (PRAH-ses) A set of actions done in a certain order.

protein (PROH-teen) An important element inside the cells of plants and animals.

protons (PROH-tonz) Particles with a positive electric charge found in the center of an atom.

symbol (SIM-bul) The letter or letters that stand for an element.

synthetic (sin-THEH-tik) Something that is not made in nature.

Index

A
atoms, 4, 7, 10, 12, 19

C
carbohydrate(s), 16

E
electrons, 4–5
element(s), 4–5, 7, 10, 17, 22
energy, 12, 15–18

F
fossil fuel(s), 18–20

G
glucose, 12–16

M
molecule, 11–12

N
neutrons, 4

O
oxygen, 10–11, 13–14, 19–20

P
photosynthesis, 12–13, 15–16, 20
protein(s), 16–17
protons, 4

S
symbol, 5
synthetic compounds, 22

Web Sites

Due to the changing nature of Internet links, PowerKids Press has developed an online list of Web sites related to the subject of this book. This site is updated regularly. Please use this link to access the list:
www.powerkidslinks.com/cin/carbon/